Hello, Family Members,

Learning to read is one of the most important accomplishments of early childhood. **Hello Reader!** books are designed to help children become skilled readers who like to read. Beginning readers learn to read by remembering frequently used words like "the," "is," and "and"; by using phonics skills to decode new words; and by interpreting picture and text clues. These books provide both the stories children enjoy and the structure they need to read fluently and independently. Here are suggestions for helping your child *before, during,* and *after* reading:

Before

- Look at the cover and pictures and have your child predict what the story is about.
- Read the story to your child.
- Encourage your child to chime in with familiar words and phrases.
- Echo read with your child by reading a line first and having your child read it after you do.

During

- Have your child think about a word he or she does not recognize right away. Provide hints such as "Let's see if we know the sounds" and "Have we read other words like this one?"
- Encourage your child to use phonics skills to sound out new words.
- Provide the word for your child when more assistance is needed so that he or she does not struggle and the experience of reading with you is a positive one.
- Encourage your child to have fun by reading with a lot of expression . . . like an actor!

After

- Have your child keep lists of interesting and favorite words.
- Encourage your child to read the books over and over again. Have him or her read to brothers, sisters, grandparents, and even teddy bears. Repeated readings develop confidence in young readers.
- Talk about the stories. Ask and answer questions. Share ideas about the funniest and most interesting characters and events in the stories.

I do hope that you and your child enjoy this book.

—Francie Alexander
   Reading Specialist,
   Scholastic's Learning Ventures

*For Grandma Roz and
Granny Rose, who were all
about the spring, with love forever
—S.B.*

*For my mother, who also
needs a little help waking up!
All my love
—P.C.*

*To Karen, Emma, and Dewey
—M.S.*

Text copyright © 2000 by Samantha Berger and Pamela Chanko.
Illustrations copyright © 2000 by Melissa Sweet.
All rights reserved. Published by Scholastic Inc.
SCHOLASTIC, HELLO READER, CARTWHEEL BOOKS and associated logos
are trademarks and/or registered trademarks of Scholastic Inc.

Library of Congress Cataloging-in-Publication Data

Berger, Samantha and Chanko, Pamela.
    It's spring! / by Samantha Berger and Pamela Chanko; illustrated by Melissa Sweet.
    p. cm. — (Hello reader! Level 2)
  "Cartwheel books."
  Summary: A rabbit, deer, and other animals give each other the message that spring is coming.
  ISBN 0-439-08754-6 (pbk.)
    [1. Animals Fiction. 2. Spring Fiction. 3. Stories in rhyme.]
I. Chanko, Pamela, 1968– . II. Sweet, Melissa, ill. III. Title. IV. Series.
  PZ8.3.B4555It 2000
  [E]—dc21
                                       99-41765
                                         CIP
                                         AC

10 9   02 03 04

Printed in the U.S.A.   24
First printing, April 2000

It's SPRING!

by Samantha Berger
and Pamela Chanko

Illustrated by Melissa Sweet

Hello Reader! — Level 2

SCHOLASTIC INC.

New York Toronto London Auckland Sydney
Mexico City New Delhi Hong Kong

*I*n April the robin began to sing
to tell the rabbit it was spring.

The rabbit hopped and thumped his feet

to tell the deer the air smelled sweet.

The little deer ran with the bunny

to tell the duck the sky was sunny.

The duck swam off and gave a quack

to tell the cow, "The leaves are back!"

The cow let out a long moo

to tell the horse that flowers grew.

The horse went trotting down the lane

to tell the rooster, "Watch for rain!"

The rooster gave a mighty crow

to tell the mouse, "There's no more snow!"

The mouse just made a tiny peep

to tell the birds to start to cheep.

Then all the birds began to sing
to tell the bears, "Wake up, it's spring!"